Pourquoi TALES

The Cat's Purr

Why Frog and Snake Never Play Together

The Fire Bringer

HOUGHTON MIFFLIN COMPANY BOSTON

Atlanta Dallas Geneva, Illinois Palo Alto Princeton Toronto

Acknowledgments

Ashley Bryan, *The Cat's Purr* from the text of the same title. Copyright ©1985 Ashley Bryan. Reprinted with the permission of Atheneum Publishers, Inc.

Ashley Bryan, "Why Frog and Snake Never Play Together," from *Beat the Story-Drum, Pum-Pum.* Copyright ©1980 Ashley Bryan. Reprinted with the permission of Atheneum Publishers, Inc.

The Fire Bringer: A Paiute Indian Legend retold by Margaret Hodges from a story in *The Basket Woman* by Mary Austin, published in 1904 by Houghton Mifflin Company. Text copyright ©1972 by Margaret Hodges. Illustrations copyright ©1972 by Peter Parnall. Reprinted by permission of the author and the illustrator.

"First and Last," from *All Day Long* by David McCord. Copyright ©1965, 1966 by David McCord. By permission of Little, Brown and Company.

"Why Nobody Pets the Lion at the Zoo" from *The Reason for the Pelican* by John Ciardi. Copyright ©1955. Reprinted by permission of the estate of John Ciardi.

Credits

Cover Illustration Cindy Brodie.

Illustration Jeffrey Severen: pp. 8, 9, 10, 13, 15, 16, 18, 21, 22, 76, 77.
Melinda May Sullivan: pp. 28, 31, 32, 35, 36, 39, 42.

Photography AP/Wide World Photos: pp. 81, 82.
Matthew Wysocki: p. 78.

Printed in the U.S.A.

ISBN: 0-395-45991-5

DEFGHIJ-D-976543210/89

Why are things the way they are? Why do some animals behave the way they do? Why does a cat purr? There are many ways to answer these questions. Some answers are scientific. Some answers are imaginative. Imaginative answers may be told in stories and myths passed down from one generation to another. These tales are often called pourquoi tales. The word *pourquoi* is French. It is pronounced *poor* ***kwah*** and means "why."

In the following pourquoi tales, you will discover several different things about animals. Are there things about animals that make *you* want to ask "Pourquoi?"

Table of Contents

The Cat's Purr

by Ashley Bryan

Once upon a time, Cat and Rat were the best of friends. Uh-huh, uh-huh, they really were! They lived in huts right next to each other. And since Rat liked to copy Cat, their huts matched.

Cat planted a coconut palm tree by his hut. Rat planted one, too.

Cat wove a straw mat for the corner of his hut. Rat wove one, too. When Rat visited Cat, he'd sit on Cat's mat; and on visits to Rat, Cat sat on Rat's mat.

Cat made a bamboo flute and played sweet tunes.

"Let me play a tune, too," said Rat.

Cat let Rat play a tune, too: *too-de-loo, too-de-loo.*

Cat and Rat farmed their land together. They worked in the field each day and took good care of their vegetable patch. After work they headed home, each with his hoe.

"When the vegetables are ready, let's have a big feast," said Cat one day.

"A grand party with dancing and singing," said Rat, "uh-huh, uh-huh!"

They laughed and talked of the feast as they walked along singing, "Ho, for a feast and hi, for a song."

One night, Cat's old uncle visited and brought Cat a present. Cat unwrapped the package. There, inside, was a small drum, the smallest drum Cat had ever seen.

"It's a cat drum," the old uncle said, "passed down in the family. Now it's just for you."

"It's so small. Can I play it?" asked Cat.

"Oh, yes!" said Cat's uncle. "It's small, and there's a special way to play it. Don't rap it or beat it or poke it, or you won't get a good sound. Stroke it gently and listen."

Cat stroked the drum gently. The drum went: *purrum, purrum.*

"Oh, meow!" said Cat. "How soothing, how beautiful!"

"Take good care of the drum," Cat's old uncle said as he was leaving. "Remember now, don't rap it or beat it or tap it or poke it. Just stroke it gently. And don't let anyone else play it."

The next morning Rat called on Cat, as he always did, on the way to work in the fields. He tapped on Cat's hut door: *rap-a-tap tap, rap-a-tap tap.*

Purrum, purrum, purrum came the sound from inside Cat's hut. Rat had never heard such music before. He opened Cat's door and went in. There sat Cat on his bed, playing a small drum.

"Pit-tap-a-la-pat," said Rat. "What a big, sweet sound and from such a small drum! It's so small you could swallow it whole! Squeek-eek, play it, Cat, uh-huh!"

Purrum, purrum, purrum, played Cat. *Purrum, purrum, purrum.*

Rat twirled about. He hummed and kicked up his feet to the purrum, purrum beat until Cat stopped drumming.

"Me now!" Rat cried.

"Oh no!" said Cat. "Mee-ow! This is a Cat family drum from my uncle."

"Pit-tap-a-la-pat," said Rat. "So what? I made my hut like yours, squeak, squee-eee. I played in the shade of your coconut tree; I sat on your mat, drank coconut milk, too. I played your flute, *too-de-loo, too-de-loo.*"

"That was different, Rat," Cat said. "My uncle said no one else plays this Cat drum. Anyway, this is not a time for drumming. Let's go to work in the fields."

Cat set the drum down on the bed.

"I must think of a good plan so that I can play Cat's drum," Rat thought. "I'll need time to think."

"I'm hungry," Rat said. "Squee-eek! If I'm to work in the fields, I've got to eat food first. I'll faint if I go without breakfast."

Cat cooked cornmeal mush and served Rat. Rat ate, but he couldn't keep his eyes off the drum. It still sang in his ears, *purrum, purrum.* His fingers itched to play it.

Rat ate slowly, bowl after bowl of cornmeal mush. Still not one good drum-playing plan popped into his head. He dawdled so long over the breakfast that it was tea time when he finished. His stomach was as tight as a drum.

"It's tea time," Rat said. "Squee-eek, and I'm still hungry. We'll work better after tea, Cat. Don't you agree?"

"Meow, I'm not hungry now," said Cat. "How can you still be hungry after swallowing so much mush?"

"It just wasn't enough mush, I guess," said Rat.

"Oh, meow," said Cat, and he served Rat the tea. "Now don't get sick. Remember, we have lots of work to do for our feast."

"Sick!" Rat thought. "That's it!"

Cat had given Rat the idea he needed. Now he knew just what to do.

"Pit-tap-a-la-pat," Rat cried as he pushed aside his cup and plate. "I'm full now and ready for work. Squee-eek."

"Pit-tap-a-la-po," Cat cried. "Here's your hoe. Meow, let's go!"

Rat was almost to the door when he moaned and fell to the ground. He turned and tossed at Cat's feet.

"Ooo-ooo," Rat groaned. "My belly's hurting me too bad. Squeak, Squee-eek."

"I knew you'd be sick," Cat said.

Cat helped Rat to his feet.

"Ah, poor Rat. Don't lie on the floor. Come, lie on my bed."

"Ooo-ooo. Thank you. Squeek-eek, ooo-ooo."

Cat put Rat to bed and spread a coverlet over him.

"Rest," said Cat. "When your belly is cool, come and help me till the fields."

"I will come, oh-ooo, when I'm well. We two do work so well together. Oh-ooo, oh-ooo!"

Though Rat wailed well, he was not ill at all, uh-uh! He stretched out on Cat's bed till his toes touched the drum. His plan was working, and he felt happy.

Cat left Rat to rest and set out for their vegetable patch. Rat waited until he was sure that Cat had reached the field. Then Rat threw off the coverlet, sat up and began to sing:

"Pit-tap-a-la-pat
Pit-tap-a-la-ping
Eat off Cat's food
And don't pay a thing."

Rat reached for Cat's drum and hugged it.

"I'd rather hug a drum than do hum-drum hoeing," Rat laughed. "Now it's my turn to play Cat's drum."

Rat had danced while Cat drummed, so he had not learned Cat's secret of how best to beat it.

Rat tapped the drum, no purrum. Rat beat the drum, no purrum. He poked it, no-no, no purrum! Instead of hugging Cat's drum now, Rat was so mad he could have pounded it. But by chance he stroked it. And there it was: *purrum, purrum, purrum.*

"Pit-tap-a-la-pat!" cried Rat. "What a thing, this drum. Rap it, tap it, beat it, poke it—no loud, sweet purrum. But when you stroke it—*purrum, purrum, purrum.*"

Far off in the field, Cat heard the sound. It was his drum—*purrum, purrum, purrum.* He dropped his hoe and ran toward his hut.

Rat saw Cat coming across the field. Quickly he replaced the drum at the foot of the bed. He stretched out and drew the coverlet up to his chin. He closed his eyes and pretended to be asleep. Cat ran into the room, shook Rat awake and shouted:

"Pit-tap-a-la-pat
Pit-tap-a-la-pum
Who's that knocking
On my drum?"

"I fell asleep," said Rat. "I didn't hear a thing. Squee-eek, oh-ooo! My belly's hurting me too bad."

"You mean your belly's not cool yet, Rat?" Cat asked. "Well, lie down, but keep your eyes open."

"I will do as well as I can, Cat, even though I'm ill."

Cat set out alone to till the fields.

And Rat could hardly wait to play the drum again. When Cat was well out of sight, he sat up in bed and sang:

"Pit-tap-a-la-pat
Pit-tap-a-la-ping
Eat off Cat's food
And don't pay a thing."

Rat shook with excitement when he took up the drum. First he hugged it, then he stroked it more lightly than

before. An even louder *purrum, purrum, purrum* came from the drum.

As Cat hoed a row of vegetables, he heard *purrum, purrum, purrum.* At once he dropped his hoe and headed for home.

Rat was again in bed and under the coverlet when Cat ran in. Cat shook Rat and cried:

"Pit-tap-a-la-pat
Pit-tap-a-la-pum
Who's that knocking
On my drum?"

"You make my belly ache more when you shake me up so," said Rat. "Oo-ooo, my belly's hurting me too bad. I didn't hear a thing."

"But, Rat, I tell you someone is knocking on my drum. I hear it in the field—*purrum, purrum, purrum.* Come now, help me, Rat."

"How can I?" said Rat. "I'm lying down, and my belly is hurting me."

"Stay in my bed till your belly's cool. But keep your eyes open. Find out who's knocking on my drum and tell me."

Cat left and closed the door. This time though, Cat didn't go far along the path to the field. He doubled back, ducked down and crept to the side of the hut. There he climbed in through the kitchen window and hid under the table.

When Rat thought that Cat was far out of sight, he sat right up in bed.

"What's this?" Cat asked himself. "Maybe Rat's belly is cool now."

He watched Rat from the hiding place under the table. He saw Rat take up the drum. Cat did not move. Rat began to sing:

"I fooled Cat once"

Cat kept quiet.

"I fooled Cat twice"

Cat blinked his eyes.

"I play Cat's drum"

Cat's ears twitched.

"Purrum, purrum, purrum."

"Drop that drum, Rat," cried Cat. "I've caught you at it. Mee-ow."

"You haven't caught me yet," cried Rat.

Rat dodged and scampered down as Cat leaped onto the bed.

So Cat jumped off the bed and trapped Rat in the corner.

All Rat saw was Cat's wide-open mouth and Cat's very sharp teeth. And that gave Rat a new idea.

As Cat flung himself at Rat, Rat plunged the drum into Cat's open mouth and fled.

Cat fell against the bed. He gulped and swallowed. Down went the drum. To his surprise, Cat realized that instead of

swallowing Rat, he had swallowed his drum.

Cat stroked his stomach to settle the drum. A muffled sound came from within: *purrum, purrum, purrum.*

Rat ran out of Cat's hut and past his own. He didn't stop to pack a thing, uh-uh! He kept on going, and he didn't look back. By the time Cat finally ran out of doors, Rat was long gone.

"That's that for our vegetable feast," Cat cried. "If I ever catch that Rat, I'll feast on him. Meow!"

Since that day, Cat carries his drum safely within. You can't fool Cat anymore with belly cool this and belly cool that. Uh-uh! Cat always knows now who's playing his drum because Cat alone chooses whom he'll let play.

If you're kind to Cat, he'll let you play his drum. Remember, though, don't tap it or beat it, don't rap it or poke it. Just stroke Cat gently, very, very gently. Uh-huh, uh-huh!

Listen now. Can you hear Cat purring—*purrum, purrum, purrum?*

That's cat's drum!

Purrum, purrum, purrum.

Discussion

1. Cat and Rat had thought they were good friends. Were they? Why?

2. Why does Rat want to play the drum? Is that a good reason? Why? Why won't Cat let him play the drum? Is that a fair reason? Why?

3. If Rat had known that playing with Cat's drum would wreck their friendship, do you think he would still have done it? Why do you think that?

Why Frog and Snake Never Play Together

Why Frog and Snake Never Play Together

by Ashley Bryan

Mama Frog had a son. Mama Snake also had a son. One morning both children went out to play.

Mama Snake called after her child:

"Watch out for big things with sharp claws and teeth that gnaw. Don't lose your way in the bush, baby, and be back to the burrow before dark."

"Clawsangnaws," sang Snake as he went looping through the grass. "Beware of the Clawsangnaws."

Mama Frog called after her son:

"Watch out for things that peck or bite. Don't go into the bush alone, dear. Don't fight, and get home before night."

"Peckorbite," sang Frog as he went hopping from stone to stone. "Beware of the Peckorbite!"

Snake was singing his Clawsangnaws song, and Frog was singing of Peckorbites when they met along the way. They had never met before.

"Who are you?" asked Frog. "Are you a Peckorbite?" and he prepared to spring out of reach.

"Oh no! I'm Snake, called by my Mama 'Snakeson': I'm slick, lithe and slithery. Who are you? Are you a Clawsangnaws?" and he got ready to move, just in case.

"No no! I'm Frog, called by my Mama 'Frogchild.' I'm hip, quick and hoppy."

They stood and stared at each other, then they said together:

"You don't look anything like me."

Their eyes brightened. They did not look alike, that's true, but some of their customs were alike. Both knew what to do when two say the same thing at the same time.

They clasped each other, closed their eyes and sang:

"You wish a wish
I'll wish a wish, too;
May your wish and my wish
Both come true."

Each made a wish then let go.

Just then a fly flew by, right past Frog's eyes. Flip! Out went his tongue as he flicked in the fly.

A bug whizzed past Snake's nose. Flash! Snake flicked out his tongue and caught the bug.

They looked in admiration at each other and smiled. The two new friends now knew something of what each other could do. They felt at ease with each other, like old friends.

"Let's play!" said Frog.

"Hey!" said Snake, "that was my wish. Let's play in the bush."

"The bush! In the bush!" cried Frog. "That was my wish. If you go with me, it's all right 'cause Mama said I shouldn't go alone."

Frog and Snake raced to the bush and started playing games.

"Watch this," said Frog. He crouched down and counted, "One a fly, two a fly, three a fly, four!"

He popped way up into the air, somersaulted and came down, whop!

"Can you do that, Snake?"

Snake bounded for a nearby mound to try the Frog-Hop. He got to the top of the slope, stood on the tip of his tail and tossed himself into the air. Down he came, flop! a tangle of coils. He laughed and tried again.

Sometimes Snake and Frog jumped together and bumped in midair. No matter how hard they hit, it didn't hurt. They had fun.

Then Snake said, "Watch this!" He stretched out at the top of the mound and counted, "One a bug, two a bug, three a bug, four!" Then swoosh! he slithered down the slope on his stomach.

"Try that Frog. It's called the Snake-Slither."

Frog lay on his stomach and slipped down the hill. His arms and legs flailed about as he slithered. He turned over at the bottom of the slope, *blump!* and rolled up in a lump.

Frog and Snake slithered down together, entangling as they went. Their calls and laughter could be heard all over the bush. One game led to another. They were having such a good time that the day passed swiftly. By late afternoon there were not two better friends in all the bush.

The sun was going down when Snake remembered his promise to his mother.

"I promised to be home before dark," he said.

"Me too," said Frog. "Good-bye!"

They hugged. Snake was so happy that he'd found a real friend that he forgot himself and squeezed Frog very tightly. It felt good, very, very good.

"Ow! easy!" said Frog. "Not too tight."

"Oh, sorry," said Snake loosening his hug-hold. "My! but you sure feel good, good enough to eat."

At that they burst out laughing and hugged again, lightly this time.

"I like you," said Frog. "Bye, Snake."

"Bye, Frog. You're my best friend."

"Let's play again tomorrow," they said together.

Aha! They clasped and sang once again:

"You wish a wish
I'll wish a wish, too;
May your wish and my wish
Both come true."

Off they went, Snake hopping and Frog slithering all the way home.

When Frog reached home, he knocked his knock, and Mama Frog unlocked the rock door. She was startled to see her child come slithering in across the floor.

"Now what is this, eh?" she said. "Look at you, all covered with grass and dirt."

"It doesn't hurt," said Frog. "I had fun."

"Fun? Now what is this, eh? I can tell you haven't been playing in ponds or bogs with the good frogs. Where have you been all day? You look as if you've just come out of the bush."

"But I didn't go alone, Ma. I went with a good boy. He's my best friend."

"Best friend? Now what is this, eh?" said Mama Frog. "What good boy could that be, playing in the bush?"

"Look at this trick that he taught me, Ma," said Frog-child. He flopped on his stomach and wriggled across the

floor, bungling up Mama Frog's neatly stitched lily-pad rug.

"That's no trick for a frog! Get up from there, child!" cried Mama Frog. "Now what is this, eh? Look how you've balled up my rug. Just you tell me, who was this playmate?"

"His name is Snakeson, Mama."

"Snake, son! Did you say Snake, son?"

"Yes. What's the matter, Mama?"

Mama Frog trembled and turned a pale green. She sat down to keep from fainting. When she had recovered herself, she said:

"Listen Frogchild, listen carefully to what I have to say." She pulled her son close. "Snake comes from the Snake family. They are bad people. Keep away from them. You hear me, child?"

"Bad people?" asked Frog.

"Bad, too bad!" said Mama Frog. "Snakes are sneaks. They hide poison in their tongues, and they crush you in their coils."

Frogchild gulped.

"You be sure to hop out of Snake's reach if ever you meet again. And stop this slithering foolishness. Slithering's not for frogs."

Mama Frog set the table muttering to herself: "Playing with Snake! Now what is this, eh?" She rolled a steaming ball of gleaming cornmeal onto Frogchild's plate.

"Sit down and eat your funji, child," said Mama Frog. "And remember, I'm not fattening frogs for snakes, eh?"

Snake too reached home. He rustled the braided twig hatch-cover to his home. His mother knew his rustle and undid the vine latch. Snake toppled in.

"I'm hungry, Ma," he said, hopping all about.

"Eh, eh! Do good bless you! What a sight you are!" said Mama Snake. "Just look at you. And listen to your panting and wheezing. Where have you been all day?"

"In the bush, Mama, with my new friend. We played games. See what he taught me."

Snakeson jumped up on top of the table and leaped into the air. He came down on a stool, knocking it over and entangling himself in its legs.

"Eh, eh! Do good bless you. What a dangerous game that is," said Mama Snake. "Keep it up and see if you don't break every bone in your back. What new friend taught you that?"

She bent over and untangled her son from the stool.

"My frog friend taught me that. His name's Frogchild. It's the Frog-Hop Mama. Try it. It's fun."

"Frog, child?" Mama Snake's jaws hung open showing her fangs. "Did you say Frog, child?"

"Yes," said Snakeson. "He's my best friend."

"You mean you played all day with a frog and you come home hungry?"

"He was hungry, too, Mama, after playing the Snake Slither game that I taught him."

"Eh, eh! Well do good bless you! Come, curl up here son and listen carefully to what I have to tell you."

Snakeson curled up on the stool.

"Don't you know, son, that it is the custom of our house to eat frogs? Frogs are delicious people!"

Snakeson's small eyes widened.

"Ah, for true!" said Mama Snake. "Eating frogs is the custom of our house, a tradition in our family. Hopping isn't, so cut it out, you hear me?"

"Oh, Mama," cried Snakeson. "I can't eat frogs. Frog's a friend."

"Frog a friend! Do good bless you!" said Mama Snake. "That's not natural. Now you listen to me, baby. The next time you play with Frog, jump roll and romp all you like. But when you get hungry, his game is up. Catch him and eat him!"

The next morning Snakeson was up early. He pushed off his dry-leaf cover and stretched himself. He remembered his mother's words, and the delicious feel of his frog friend when they had hugged. He was ready to go.

Mama Snake fixed her son a light breakfast of spiced insects and goldfinch eggs. Snakeson was soon on his way.

"Now don't you forget my instructions about frogs, do good bless you," Mama Snake called out after him. "And don't let me have to tell you again to watch out for big things with sharp claws and teeth that gnaw."

"Clawsangnaw," sang Snakeson. "Clawsangnaw."

He reached the bush and waited for his friend. He looked forward to fun with Frog, and he looked forward to finishing the fun with a feast of his fine frog friend. He lolled about in the sun, laughing and singing:

"You wish a wish
I'll wish a wish, too;
Can your wish and my wish
Both come true?"

The sun rose higher and higher, but Frog did not come.

"What's taking Frogchild so long?" said Snakeson. "Perhaps too much slithering has given him the bellyache. I'll go and look for him."

Snake found Frog's rock home by the pond. He rolled up a stone in his tail and knocked on the rock door.

"Anybody home?"

"Just me," answered Frogchild.

"May I come in?"

"Ah, it's you Snakeson. Sorry, my Mama's out, and she said not to open the door to anyone."

"Come on out then and let's play," said Snakeson. "I waited all morning for you in the bush."

"I can't," said Frog, "not now, anyway."

"Oh, that's too bad," said Snake. "My mother taught me a new game. I'd love to teach it to you."

"I'll bet you would," said Frog.

"You don't know what you're missing," said Snake.

"But I do know what you're missing," said Frog, and he burst out laughing.

"Aha!" said Snake. "I see that your mother has given you instructions. My mother has given me instructions too."

Snake sighed. There was nothing more to say or do, so he slithered away.

Frog and Snake never forgot that day when they played together as friends. Neither ever again had that much fun with anybody.

Today you will see them, quiet and alone in the sun, still as stone. They are deep in thought remembering that day of games in the bush, and both of them wonder:

"What if we had just kept on playing together, and no one had ever said anything?"

But from that day to this, Frog and Snake have never played together again.

You wish a wish
I'll wish a wish, too;
May your wish and my wish
Both come true.

Discussion

1. If Frogchild and Snakeson had kept their day together a secret, what do you think would have happened?

2. What do Snakeson and Frogchild teach each other when they first meet? What kinds of things have you learned from your friends?

3. What would happen if Frogchild and Snakeson play together again? Why do you think that?

The Fire Bringer
A Paiute Indian Legend

The Fire Bringer

A Paiute Indian Legend

Retold by Margaret Hodges

Illustrated by Peter Parnall

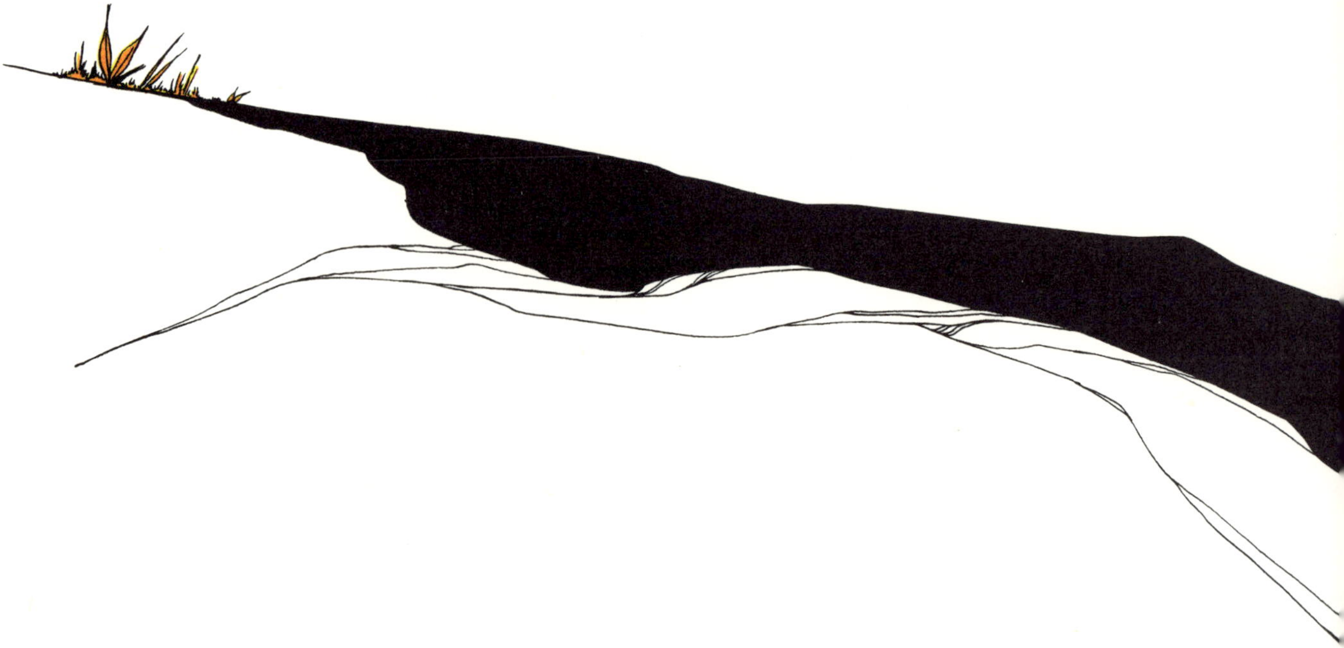

The Fire Bringer was an Indian boy. The skin of his body was dark and shining, and he had straight black locks cropped at his shoulders. He wore no clothing but a scrap of deerskin belted with a wisp of bark, and he ran free on mesa and mountain. He carried in his hand a hunting club made of a cleft stick and a rounded stone.

He lived in the long-ago time before fire was brought to the tribes, when men and beasts could talk together, and understand each other.

The Coyote, keen gray dog of the wilderness, was the Friend and Counselor of man, and when the boy went out to hunt, the Coyote ran by his side.

In the summer they saw men catching fish in the creeks with their hands. They saw women digging with sharp stones for roots to eat. In the summer they fared well.

But when winter came, the people ran shivering in the snow or huddled in caves. The boy saw that they were miserable, and he felt very unhappy.

"My people suffer and have no way to escape the cold," he said.

"I do not feel the cold," said the Coyote.

"That is because you have a fur coat," said the boy. "My people have no fur coats."

"Let them run about, then," said the Coyote. "That will keep them warm."

"They run till they are weary," the boy said. "And there are young children and old people who cannot run. Help us, O Counselor!"

"There is a way to get help," said the Coyote. "It is very hard, but you and I will take that way together. We must go to the west and bring fire from the Burning Mountain. The tribe must help too. We will need a hundred men and women, strong and swift runners."

Then he told the boy what fire was, and the boy tried to understand.

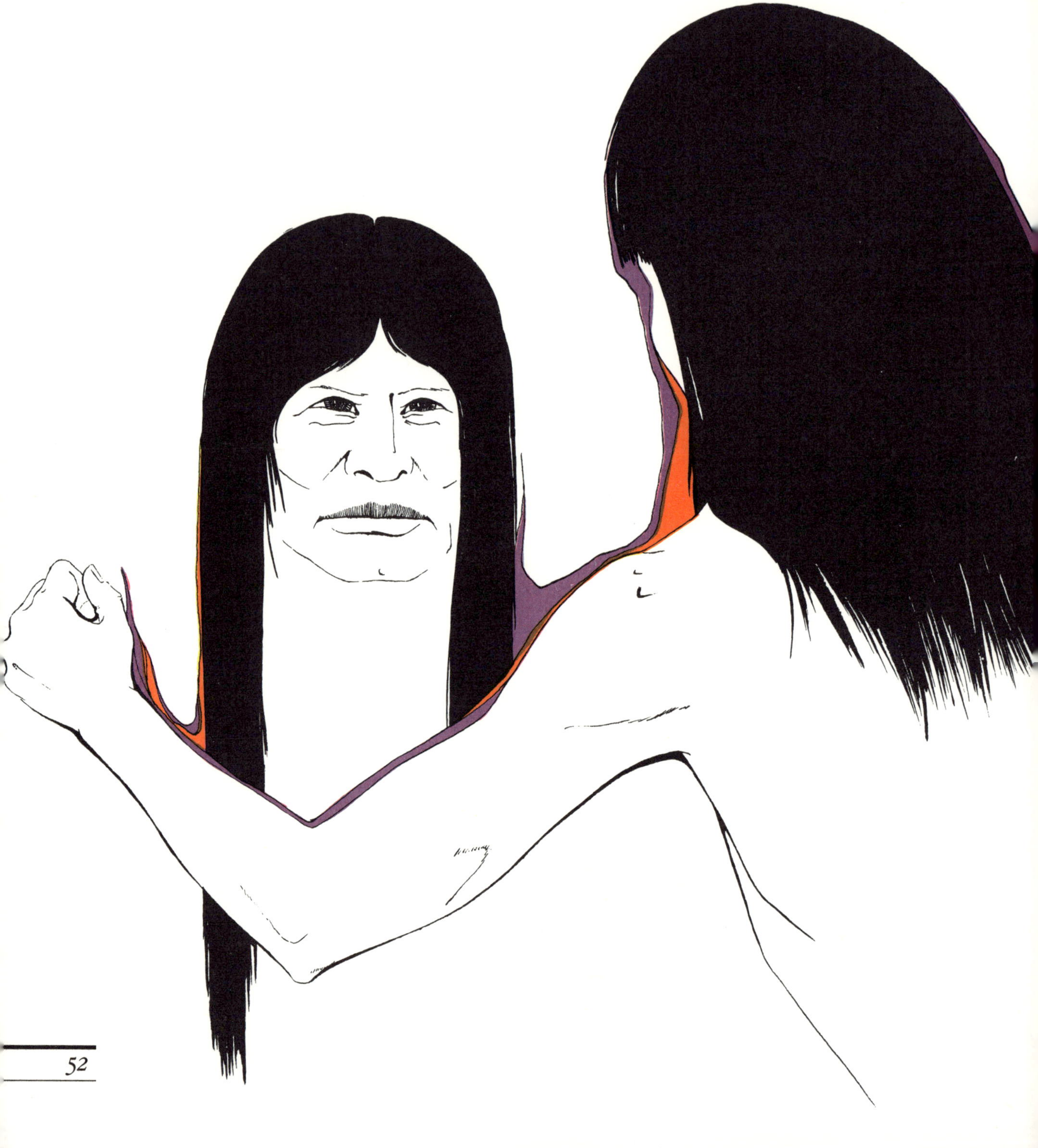

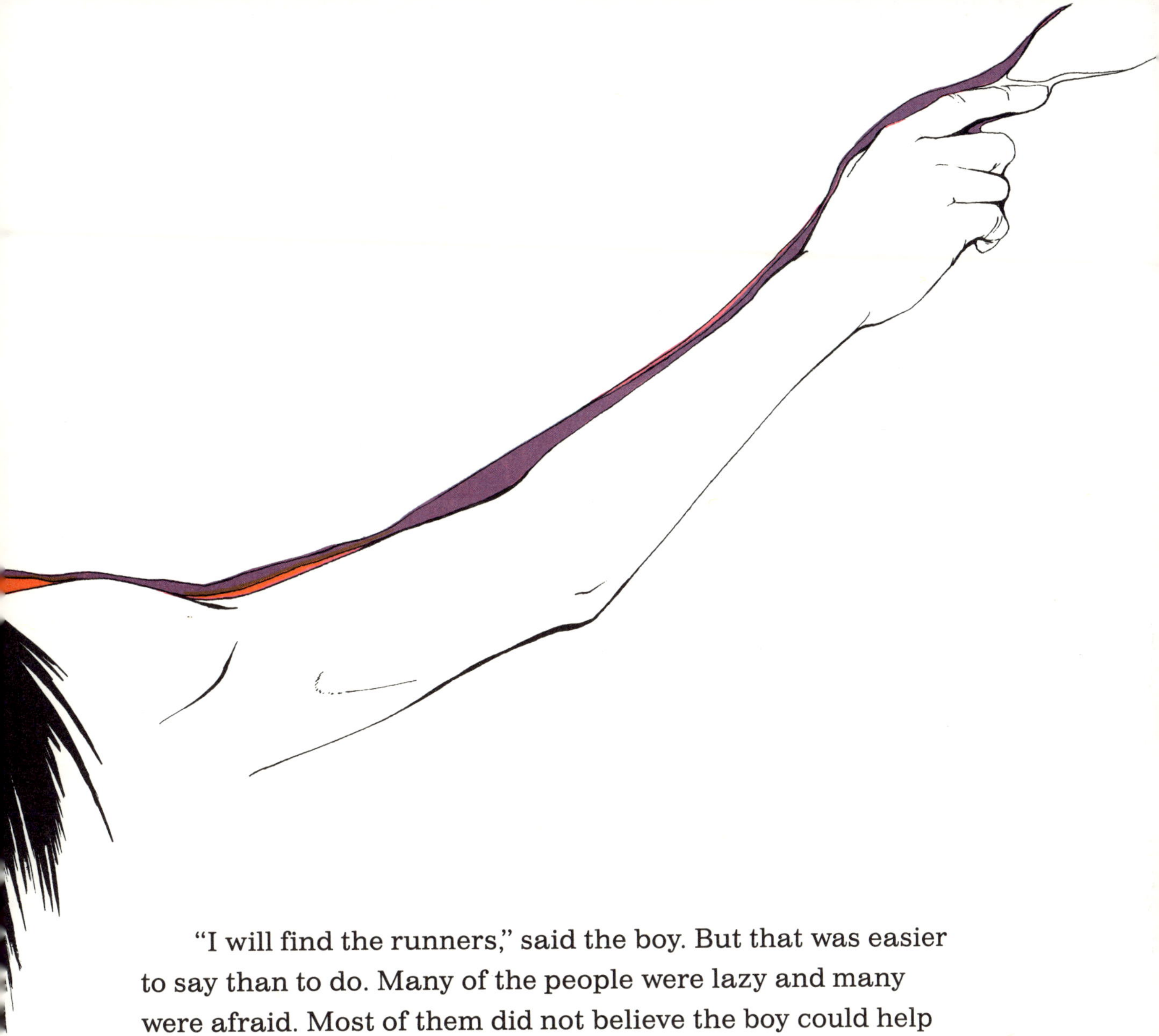

“I will find the runners,” said the boy. But that was easier to say than to do. Many of the people were lazy and many were afraid. Most of them did not believe the boy could help them, for they said, “We have never heard of fire. How can this boy know something that we do not know?”

But at last the boy talked so much about fire and the people were so miserable in the cold that they decided to do what the boy told them. A hundred men and women, the best and fastest runners, said they would go with him.

The Coyote advised them how the march should begin. He and the boy led the way. Next to them went the swiftest runners of the tribe, with the others following according to their strength and speed. They left the place of their home and went over high mountains where great jagged peaks stood up above the snow. They went down the other side of those mountains into a dark woods where the sound of the wind in the branches made them afraid. Here the Coyote stopped.

"Do not fear," he said to the people. "Take your rest."

In the morning he chose one man to stay in that place, saying, "Wait here until the fire comes."

"How will I know when I see it?" asked the man. "How does fire look?"

"It is red like a flower," said the Coyote, "but it is not a flower. You will know it when you see it." He led the tribe on toward the west.

The next night another man stayed where he was, and again the Coyote led the tribe westward. So it was at the end of each day's journey until they came to a great plain where the earth was dry and cracked and the parched grass rustled like straw. The Coyote chose a man to stay in that place.

"Rest here until the fire comes," he said. "But do not let it touch the grass. Fire can run raging through the grass and devour all before it."

"Is it a beast?" asked the man.

"No, it is not a beast," said the Coyote. "You will know it when you see it."

So they went on until only one runner was left with the boy and the Coyote. And they came to another range of hills, not so high but tumbled thickly together and covered with a thick woods.

"Stay here," said the Coyote, "until the fire comes." But the last runner asked, "Will the fire come upon me like an enemy?"

"It can be an enemy," the Coyote told him. "It is very fierce and hurtful and stays not for the asking,[1] yet if it is kept among stones and fed with small sticks, it will serve the people well and keep them warm."

---

[1]*stays not for the asking:* an unwelcome visitor.

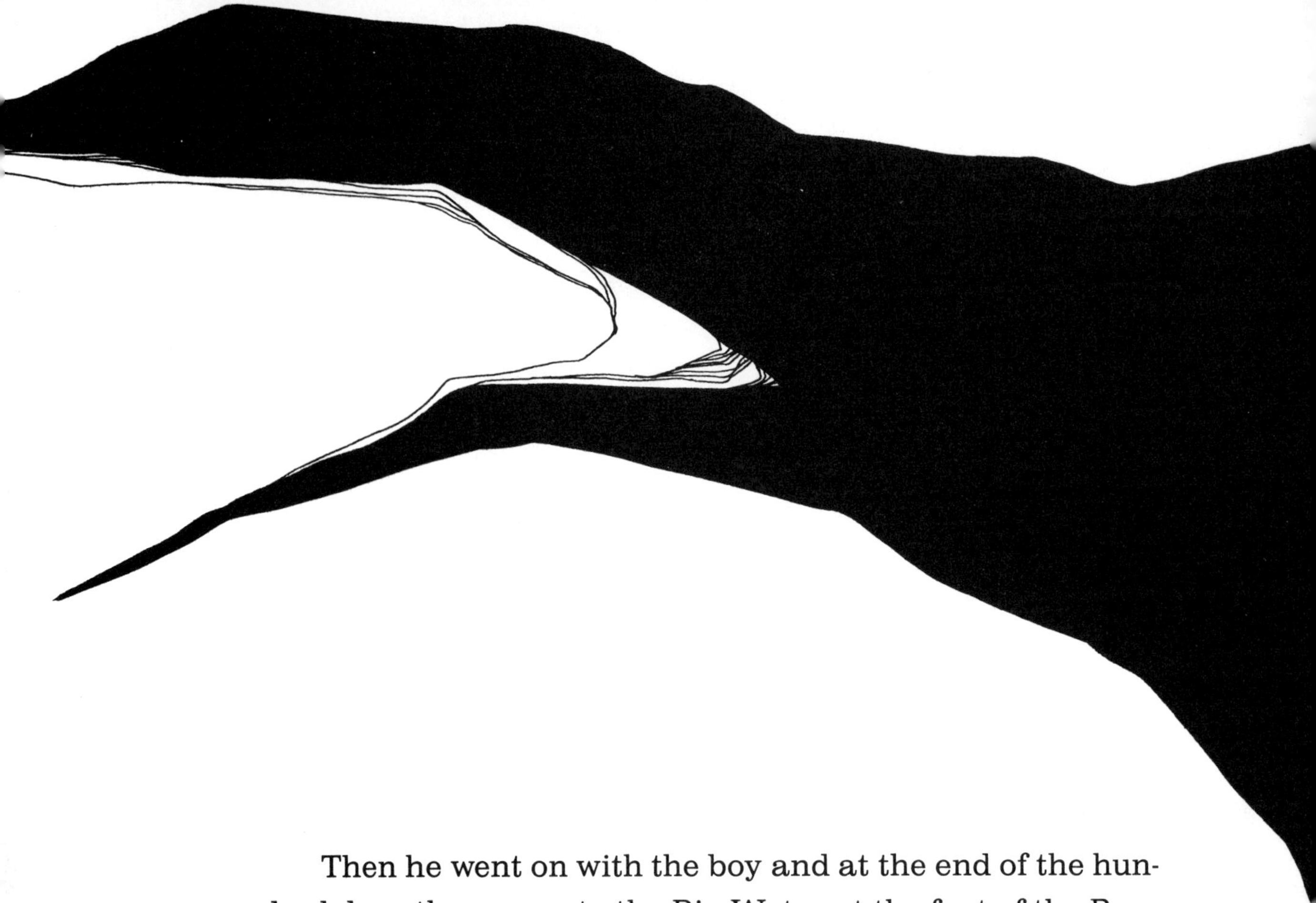

Then he went on with the boy and at the end of the hundred days they came to the Big Water at the foot of the Burning Mountain. It stood up in a high and peaked cone and the smoke of its burning rolled out and broke along the sky. By night the glare of the fire reddened the waves of the Big Water when the Fire Spirits began their dance.

"There is the fire," said the Coyote. "It has its lair inside the mountain, and the Fire Spirits guard it night and day. Stay here until I bring you a brand from the burning. Be ready and right for running, and lose no time, for I shall be far spent when I come again, and the Fire Spirits will chase me."

Then he went up the mountain, and the Fire Spirits laughed when they saw him coming. He was thin, and his coat was much the worse for his long journey. Slinking, shabby and mean he looked, as he has always looked, and it served him as well then as it serves him now. He looked like an animal of no importance, so the Fire Spirits paid him no heed.

Along in the night when they began to dance, the Coyote stole a blazing piece of wood and ran with it down the slope of the Burning Mountain.

When the Fire Spirits saw what he had done, they streamed out after him, red and angry, with a sound like a swarm of bees.

The boy saw the Coyote coming with the Fire Spirits after him. He saw the hot sparks stream back along the Coyote's sides as he carried the firebrand in his mouth and stretched forward on the trail, bright as a falling star against the dark bulk of the mountain.

Then the boy stood up in his place, clean limbed and taut for running. He heard the singing sound of the Fire Spirits behind the Coyote and the labored breath of the Counselor nearing through the dark.

The boy stood bent for the running as a bow bends to speed the arrow. The good beast panted down beside him and the brand dropped from his jaws. The boy caught it up. Out he shot on the homeward path and the Fire Spirits snapped and sung behind him. Fast as they chased him, he fled faster until he saw the next runner stand up in his place to take the firebrand from him.

So it passed from hand to hand, and the Fire Spirits tore after it through the thick woods and over the parched prairie until they came to the mountains of the snows. These they could not pass.

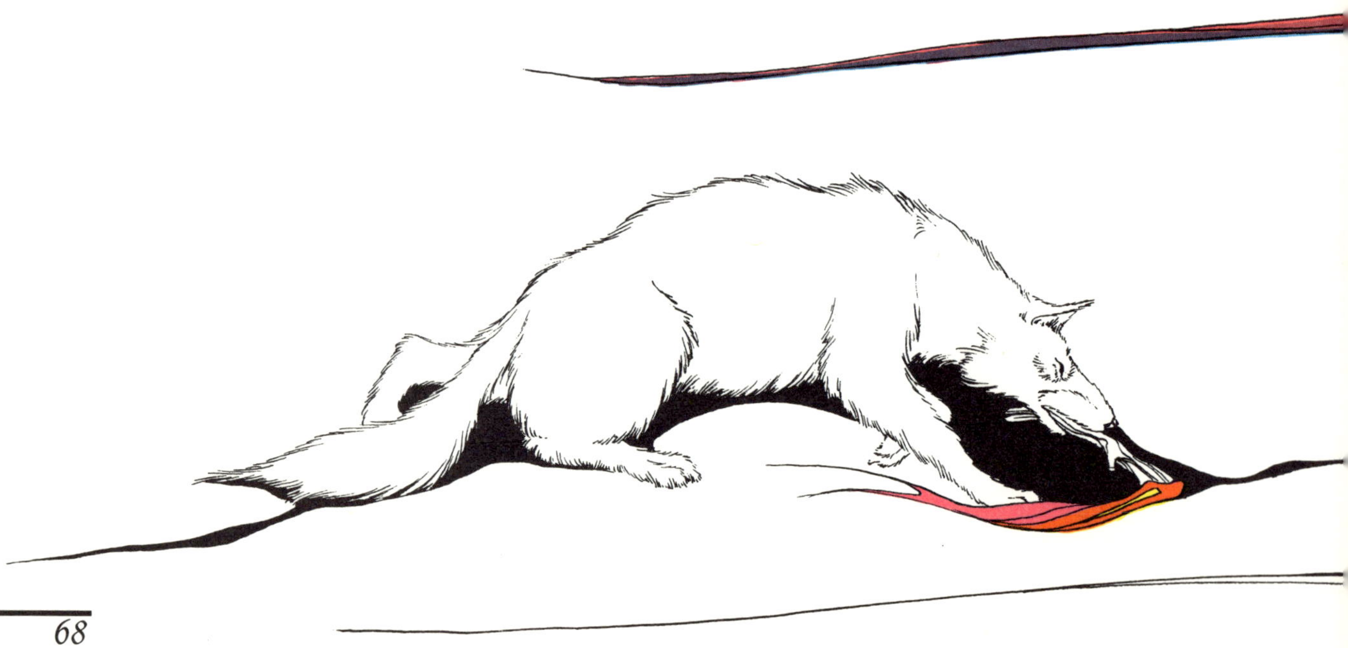

And the dark, sleek runners with the backward-streaming brand bore it forward, shining starlike in the night, glowing red through sultry noons, violet pale at twilight, until they came in safety to their own land.

Here they kept the fire among stones and fed it with small sticks as the Coyote advised, and it warmed them and cooked their food.

As for the boy, he was called the Fire Bringer while he lived. And after that, the Coyote was called the Fire Bringer, since there was no other with so good a right to the name.

And this is the sign that the tale is true. All along the Coyote's thin sides the fur is singed and yellow to this very day, as it was by the flames that blew backward from the brand when he brought it down from the Burning Mountain.

Discussion

1. When Coyote explains fire to the boy, he tries to understand. But the boy has never seen fire. Is it possible to understand something you have never seen? Give reasons for your answer.

2. How does Coyote explain fire? How would you describe fire to someone who had never seen it?

3. Why does Coyote risk his life to deliver fire to the tribes?

4. Suppose one of the runners had dropped the firebrand. Do you think Coyote could return to the mountain to steal another one? Why or why not?

Roundtable Discussion

1. Why do you think these tales came to be told?

2. Frog, Snake, Rat, and Cat each lost something in these tales. How are their losses similar? How are they different?

3. Think of the friendships in all three tales. Based on what you have read, what do *you* think makes a good friendship?

First and Last

A tadpole hasn't a pole at all,
And he *doesn't* live in a hole in the wall.

You've got it wrong: a polecat's not
A cat on a pole. And I'll tell you what:

A bullfrog's never a bull; and how
Could a cowbird possibly be a cow?

A kingbird, though, *is* a kind of king,
And he chases a crow like anything.

David McCord

Why Nobody Pets the Lion at the Zoo

The morning that the world began
The Lion growled a growl at Man.

And I suspect the Lion might
(If he'd been closer) have tried a bite.

I think that's as it ought to be
And not as it was taught to me.

I think the Lion has a right
To growl a growl and bite a bite.

And if the Lion bothered Adam,
He should have growled right back at 'im.

The way to treat a Lion right
Is growl for growl and bite for bite.

True, the Lion is better fit
For biting than for being bit.

But if you look him in the eye
You'll find the Lion's rather shy.

He really wants someone to pet him.
The trouble is: his teeth won't let him.

He has a heart of gold beneath
But the Lion just can't trust his teeth.

John Ciardi

About the Authors and Artist

Ashley Bryan Ashley Bryan was born in New York City in 1923. As a young boy, he spent a lot of his time learning to paint and draw. Bryan is very interested in African poetry, songs, and stories. He has written many books, such as *The Ox of the Wonderful Horns* and *The Dancing Granny.* Bryan says, "I like to play with sounds and words." He thinks it is a good idea to read his stories out loud.

Margaret Hodges Margaret Hodges has won many awards for her books and stories. She was born in Indiana in 1911 and often writes stories about her childhood. Her favorite stories are about the funny things that happened to her when she was growing up. She also likes to write stories about the adventures of her three sons. *The Wave* and *Lady Queen Anne* are two of her books. Hodges once had her own television show called "Tell Me a Story." When she is not writing, Hodges likes to read, travel, and work in her garden.

Peter Parnall When Peter Parnall was in school, he thought that he wanted to become an animal doctor. Instead, he decided that he would rather draw animals than operate on them! He is now a famous illustrator. Parnall was born in New York in 1939. He grew up with many animals around him. Parnall now enjoys taking long walks in the woods to watch deer and other wild creatures. While on these walks, he sometimes sketches animals for his next book. Parnall lives with his family on a farm in Maine, where they raise sheep.

David McCord David McCord was born in New York City in 1897. When he was twelve, he and his parents moved to a ranch in Oregon. The ranch had no electricity, no running water, and no oil or coal. After high school, McCord enlisted in the army. He later went to Harvard. McCord wrote poetry as a hobby. "One of the things I learned as a country boy," he said, "was to see, hear, feel and breathe the rhythm of the earth." *Far and Few: Rhymes of the Never Was and Always Is* and *The Star in the Pail* are two of his volumes of poetry for younger audiences.

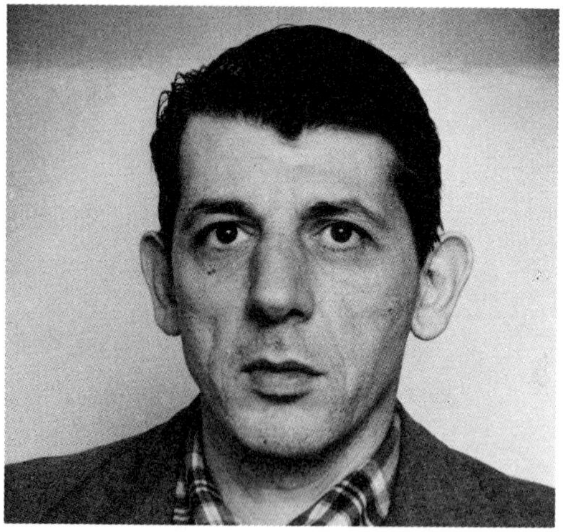

John Ciardi John Ciardi was born in Boston in 1916. He taught at several universities. In 1961 he stopped teaching so that he could write full time. He also began to write for children. Two of his books of poetry for children are *Scappy the Pup* and *I Met a Man.* Ciardi spent his life trying to make poetry popular. He spoke about poetry to bankers as well as to school children. Ciardi died in 1986.

Glossary

A

ad·mi·ra·tion (ăd´ mə´ **rā´** shən) A feeling of pleasure, wonder, respect, and approval caused by something good or beautiful: *We feel great admiration for the boy who saved the drowning baby.*

ad·vise (ăd **vīz´**) To give an opinion about what to do: *The woman advised us to save our money.*

B

bam·boo (băm **bo͞o´**) A tall grass that looks like a tree. It has hollow, woody stems that are used to make window blinds and many other things.

bamboo

bog (bôg) *or* (bŏg) A soft, wet area of land; a marsh; swamp.

brand (brănd) **1.** A name or symbol that identifies a product; a trademark. **2.** A piece of burning or charred wood, also called a **firebrand** (**fīr´** brănd´).

bulk (bŭlk) Great size, mass, or volume: *The bulk of the package made it hard to carry.*

bur·row (**bûr´** ō) *or* (**bŭr**–) A hole, tunnel, or opening dug in the ground by a small animal, such as a rabbit or a mole.

bush (bo͝osh) A woody plant that is smaller than a tree and has many branches; shrub.

C

clasp (klăsp) To grasp or hold tightly: *We clasped hands when we met.*

cleft (klĕft) Cracked or split.

coil (koil) A spiral or ring or a series of spirals or rings formed by winding: *Roll that rope into a coil.*

ă **pat** / ā **pay** / â **care** / ä **father** / ĕ **pet** / ē **be** / ĭ **pit** / ī **pie** / î **fierce** / ŏ **pot** / ō **go** / ô **paw, for** / oi **oil** / o͝o **book** / o͞o **boot** / ou **out** / ŭ **cut** / û **fur** / *th* **the** / th **thin** / hw **which** / zh **vision** / ə **ago, item, pencil, atom, circus**

coun·sel·or (**koun´** sə lər) *or* (–slər) A person who advises or guides.

cov·er·let (**kŭv´**ər lĭt) A bedspread.

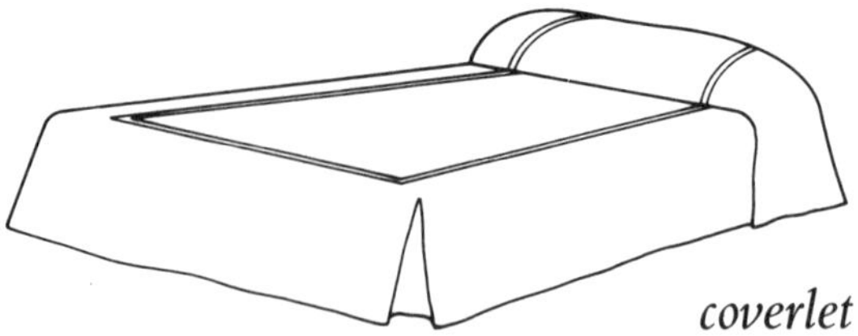

coverlet

cropped (krŏpt) **1.** Having the tops or outer parts cut off. **2.** Cut off short.

crouch (krouch) To bend low; stoop or squat.

cus·tom (**kŭs´** təm) Something people do that is widely accepted or has become a tradition: *Shaking hands when meeting someone is an old custom.*

D

daw·dle (**dô´** dəl) To take more time than is needed: *I dawdled on my way to school and was ten minutes late.*

de·vour (dĭ **vour´**) To swallow or eat eagerly: *The dog devoured its dinner in no time.*

dodge (dŏj) To avoid by moving quickly out of the way: *I dodged the snowballs thrown at me.*

E

ease (ēz) Freedom from worry, pain, or trouble; comfort: *I felt at ease with my new friends.*

en·tan·gle (ĕn **tăng´** gəl) To become snarled, mixed, or twisted together: *Don't entangle the fishing line.*

ex·tinct (ĭk **stĭngkt´**) No longer existing in living form: *The dodo bird has been extinct for hundreds of years.*

F

fare (fâr) To get along; do: *How have you fared with your project?*

fierce (fîrs) Wild and savage; dangerous: *Tigers can be fierce animals.*

flail (flāl) To wave or lash wildly;

to thrash: *The snake flailed angrily when I held it down with a stick.*

fling (flĭng) **flung** To throw hard; hurl: *The pitcher flung the ball at the batter.*

G

glare (glâr) **1.** An angry stare. **2.** A bright, unpleasant light. *The glare from the lamp hurts my eyes.*

gnaw (nô) To bite and chew over and over: *The mouse gnawed at the hard cheese.*

H

hoe (hō) A gardening tool with a flat blade set at the end of a long handle. A hoe is used for loosening soil and for weeding.

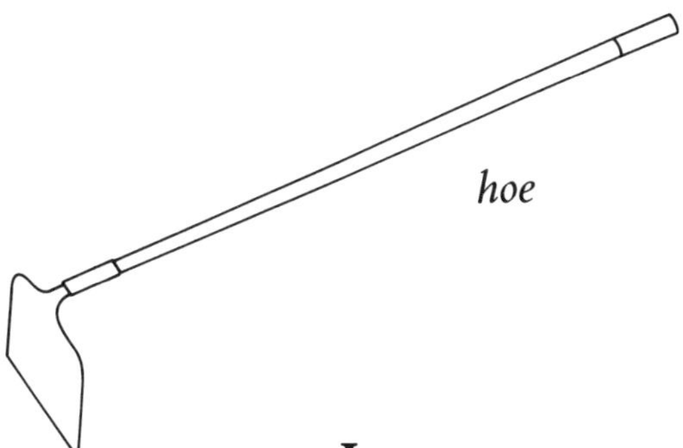

I

itch (ĭch) **1.** To have, cause, or cause to have a tickling feeling in the skin. **2.** To have a strong, restless desire: *The coach was itching to start the game.*

J

jag·ged (jăg′ ĭd) Having notches or points; sharp, rough and uneven: *A jagged piece of glass cut my foot.*

K

keen (kēn) Very quick or sensitive, especially in seeing, hearing, tasting, or smelling.

L

la·bored (lā′ bərd) Moving slowly and with effort: *His slow, labored running made him lose the race.*

lair (lâr) The den or home of a wild animal.

lithe (līth) Smooth and graceful in motion: *The young dancer was very lithe.*

locks (lŏks) The hair of the head: *The child pulled her cap over her curly locks.*

loll (lŏl) To sit or lie in a relaxed or lazy way.

loop (lo͞op) To make into a circular path or pattern.

M

me·sa (**mā´** sə) A hill with steep sides and a broad, flat top.

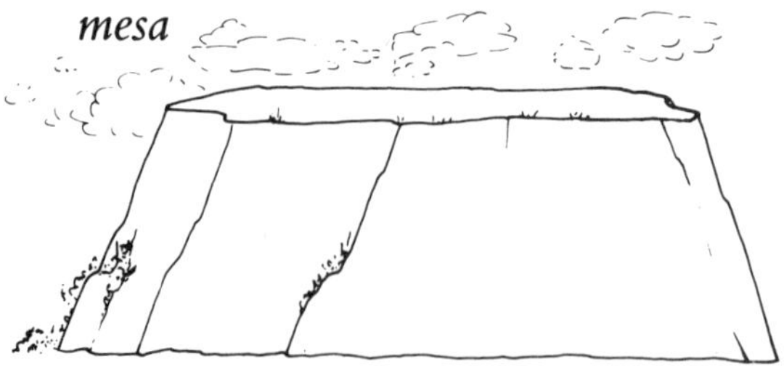

mesa

mis·er·a·ble (**mĭz´** ər ə bəl) **1.** Very unhappy. **2.** Causing real unhappiness or discomfort: *We had miserable weather last winter.*

muf·fled (**mŭf´** əld) **1.** Wrapped up in clothing or coverings. **2.** Softened or deadened to make less loud: *We could barely hear the muffled voices from the next room.*

P

parched (pärcht) Very dry, usually because of extreme heat: *The hot sun turned our bean stalks into parched weeds.*

plunge (plŭnj) To thrust suddenly and with force: *The farmer plunged the pitchfork into the hay.*

R

rus·tle (**rŭs´** əl) A soft fluttering or crackling sound: *We heard the rustle of the leaves in the wind.*

S

singed (sĭnjd) Burned slightly; scorched.

slink·ing (**slĭng´** kĭng) Moving in a secret, sneaking way, as from guilt or fear.

sli·ther·y (**slĭ***th*´ ər ē) Able to move or moving along by gliding: *The slithery eel slipped through the reeds in the river.*

som·er·sault (**sŭm´**ər sôlt) To roll the body in a complete circle, heels over head.

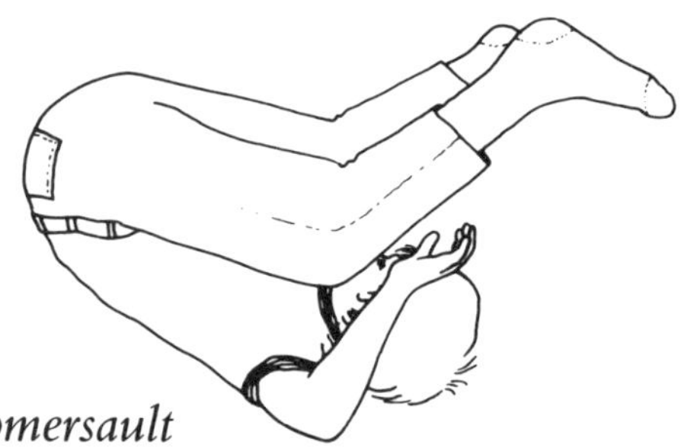

somersault

sooth·ing (**sōō´** *th*ĭng) Bringing relief or comfort.

ă pat / ā pay / â care / ä father / ĕ pet / ē be / ĭ pit / ī pie / î fierce / ŏ pot / ō go / ô paw, for / oi oil / ŏŏ book / ōō boot / ou out / ŭ cut / û fur / *th* the / th thin / hw which / zh vision / ə ago, item, pencil, atom, circus

sul·try (**sŭl′** trē) Very hot and humid: *We slept outdoors on the sultry nights of summer.*

T

taut (tôt) Pulled or drawn tight: *Pull the net taut so it won't sag in the middle.*

till (tĭl) To prepare land for growing crops by plowing and fertilizing.

twi·light (**twī′** līt′) The time at dawn or sunset when the sun is below the horizon but there is a little light in the sky.

twitch (twĭch) To move or cause to move with a quick jerk.

W

wail (wāl) To make a long, loud cry of grief, sadness, or pain: *The lost child wailed until he saw his mother.*

wea·ry (**wîr′** ē) Needing rest; tired.

wisp (wĭsp) **1.** A small bunch or strand. **2.** A thin streak: *A wisp of smoke came out the chimney.*

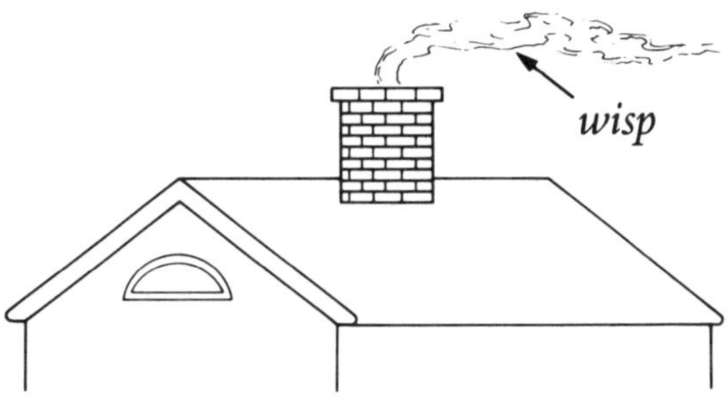